ALL THINGS BRIGHT AND BEAUTIFUL

A CHESHIRE STUDIO BOOK

NORTH-SOUTH BOOKS

NEW YORK · LONDON

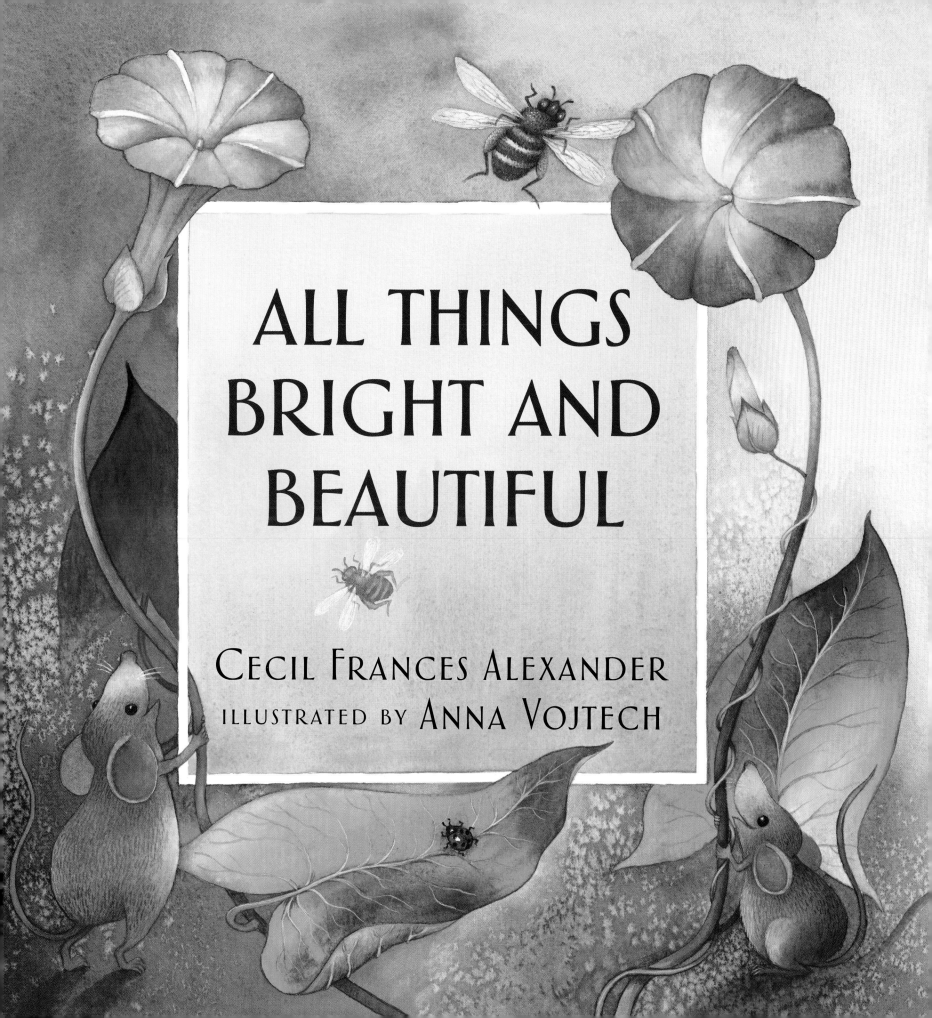

ALL THINGS BRIGHT AND BEAUTIFUL

Cecil Frances Alexander

ILLUSTRATED BY Anna Vojtech

ALL THINGS BRIGHT AND BEAUTIFUL,

ALL CREATURES GREAT AND SMALL,

ALL THINGS WISE AND WONDERFUL,

THE LORD GOD MADE THEM ALL.

EACH LITTLE FLOWER THAT OPENS,

Each little bird that sings,

HE MADE THEIR GLOWING COLORS,

HE MADE THEIR TINY WINGS.

THE PURPLE-HEADED MOUNTAIN,

THE RIVER RUNNING BY,

THE SUNSET AND THE MORNING,

THAT BRIGHTENS UP THE SKY.

THE COLD WIND IN THE WINTER,

THE PLEASANT SUMMER SUN,

THE RIPE FRUITS IN THE GARDEN,

HE MADE THEM EVERY ONE.

HE GAVE US EYES TO SEE THEM,

AND LIPS THAT WE MIGHT TELL,

HOW GREAT IS GOD ALMIGHTY,

WHO HAS MADE ALL THINGS WELL.

In memory of my mother —A.V.

A CHESHIRE STUDIO BOOK
Published in the United States by North-South Books Inc., New York.
Published simultaneously in Great Britain, Canada, Australia, and New Zealand in 2004
by North-South Books, an imprint of Nord-Süd Verlag AG, Gossau Zürich, Switzerland.

Library of Congress Cataloging-in-Publication Data is available.
A CIP catalogue record for this book is available from The British Library.

ISBN 0-7358-1892-4 (TRADE EDITION)
1 3 5 7 9 HC 10 8 6 4 2
ISBN 0-7358-1893-2 (LIBRARY EDITION)
1 3 5 7 9 LE 10 8 6 4 2
Printed in Italy

For more information about our books, and the authors and artists
who create them, visit our web site: www.northsouth.com